The Mother Goose Diaries

The Mother Goose Diaries

by Mother Goose

with Chris Colfer

LITTLE, BROWN AND COMPANY

NEW YORK   BOSTON

Little, Brown and Company

Hachette Book Group
1290 Avenue of the Americas, New York, NY 10104
Visit us at lb-kids.com

Little, Brown and Company is a division of Hachette Book Group, Inc.
The Little, Brown name and logo are trademarks of Hachette Book Group, Inc.

The publisher is not responsible for websites (or their content)
that are not owned by the publisher.

First Edition: November 2015

ISBN 978-0-316-38332-5

Library of Congress Control Number: 2015948582

10 9 8 7 6 5 4 3 2 1

RRD-C

Printed in the United States of America

To Lester, for being the best gander a gal could ask for.
Your landing technique still needs work.

Forewarning Foreword

W ell, the time has come. The confidentiality
agreements have expired, the cease-and-desist
letters have stopped coming in, the dynasties I've
been avoiding are dying out, and all the old mob
bosses I owe money to are behind bars. Look out,
world; *Mother Goose is finally publishing a memoir!*

I've never been a big fan of autobiographies. If
I wanted to hear a bunch of whiny stories from
insignificant, attention-seeking know-it-alls, I'd just
have lunch with Little Miss Muffet. It takes something
special to capture my attention. I'm talking unbelievable
adventures with remarkable people, fascinating places in
chaotic times, unusual predicaments and sequences of

events, and highly questionable evidence to back up the author's accountability. I guess that's why I decided to reread my own diary!

Boy, am I glad I kept one! I had forgotten most of the crazy shenanigans I got into over the years. That's what one too many pub brawls with talking animals and late-night ragers with enchanted silverware will do to your memory.

It's been a hoot reliving some of my best and worst moments. So entertaining, in fact, I felt guilty *not* sharing it with the rest of the world. It won't do anyone any good if I keep them to myself, and Lester is tired of hearing them over and over again. By popular demand, here is a selection of my favorite memories plucked straight from the fading parchment of my crumbling diary. (You know you're old when you've outlived leather.)

Now, just like everything I'm involved with, this diary should come with a warning. People tend to be picky when it comes to "history," so if you're going to be a snob about "accuracy," find something else to read. And if there are any so-called "scholars" out there who doubt me, let me be very clear: I was there, I know what I saw, and I know what I lived through. If my memories contradict the history you've been taught or the history you teach, that's not my problem.

Just like they say, *"History is invented by those who outdrank the other witnesses."* Or maybe I'm the one who said that? Anyhoo, I'm sure all your questions will be answered in the pages ahead. Enjoy!

100 DA (DRAGON AGE)

Dear Diary,

Today marks the hundredth anniversary of the dragons taking over the planet. It also happens to be my thirteenth birthday, and it's the worst birthday I've ever had. Two months ago Mom and Dad ran off to pursue their dreams of becoming musicians. They said they wanted a better life for me than one on the road, so they sent me to live with the fairies in the Fairy Palace.

Sometimes living with the fairies feels like I'm living in a glittery, smiley, rainbow cult. Everyone in the Fairy Kingdom is obsessed with white magic and doing good deeds. I'm like the black sheep of the

Fairy Palace, and they hate me for it. They're always teasing me in the halls and throwing crumpled up pieces of paper at me during magic lessons. I wish Mom and Dad had left me with the trolls and goblins—at least I wouldn't get into trouble for putting a bully into a headlock there.

It's been really hard making a friend here, hence why I've started journaling. There's one girl who's a little older than me who I guess is okay. Everyone really likes her a lot around here; they say she'll be running the joint when she gets older. She really likes me for some reason and has been looking out for me. I don't know her name, but she stands up for me every time she sees someone picking on me.

She was the only person who remembered it was my birthday today. She made me a cake, but then lectured me about how much of it I was eating.

"Careful," she said. "You'll make yourself sick."

"Don't mother me," I said. "We're practically the same age."

"I don't mean to *mother* you, but someone has

to look out for you," she said. "Consider me your *godmother* while you live with the fairies."

"You want to be my *fairy godmother*?" I asked.

"Fairy godmother?" she said and scrunched up her nose. "That sounds silly."

It was the only time I had seen her dislike something, so naturally I had to tease her about it. "Too late, that's what I'll be calling you from this moment on!"

The "fairy godmother" just laughed. "Whatever it takes to be your friend," she said.

I've never been used to *kindness*. It's always given me a weird feeling in the pit of my stomach, just like mermaid stew.

"Why are you so nice to me?" I asked. "All the other fairies can't stand me, so why are *you* trying to be my friend?"

"I can't explain why, but I've always loved taking care of people. It's sort of a hobby," she said. "What do you do for fun?"

"I like playing cards and picking the locks of

liquor cabinets," I said. "So I don't think I'm the kind of girl you want to be friends with."

"Are you kidding? That's *exactly* the kind of friend I want!" she said. "You're different, and different is good! The more different you have in your life, the more exciting it is! People around here don't understand that. I'm so bored of all these perfect and colorful fairies flying around—they're no fun! I'd give anything to do something thrilling and spontaneous!"

"I know what you mean," I said. "I've been thinking about sneaking away from the Fairy Palace and capturing a dragon! Want to come with me? It could be the thrilling and spontaneous thing you're looking for."

Her eyes lit up like it was the best idea she had ever heard. "Let's go!"

I never did catch her real name, but I think this "fairy godmother" girl might be the closest thing I have to a friend. Maybe my birthday wasn't such a bad day after all.

100 AD (After Dragons)

Dear Diary,

It's been one hundred years since the dragons went extinct, and I'm starting to miss those scaly suckers. Don't get me wrong: Things were terrible while they were in existence. Everything was burnt to a crisp! The air was always filled with smoke! Peasants were constantly running for their lives— even when they didn't need to be! The dragons made them so paranoid, they ran in circles around their villages all day, just in case one attacked it. No one knew how to relax with those overgrown reptiles flying around.

It was a lot of work getting rid of them, but

thankfully the fairies and I managed. Since then, we've tried restoring some sense into the kingdoms. But I can't help wondering if getting rid of the dragons was a good idea. Things have become so dull I'm starting to go stir-crazy!

Obviously I don't miss getting burned by their breath or whipped by their tails or the constant pandemonium they caused, but at least we had some fun slaying them! Sure, it was a dangerous and scary time, but it was *stimulating.* Not to mention all the money I made from wrestling the smaller ones in sold-out arenas.

Nowadays, we're so hit up for entertainment we obsess over every ditz who needs a rescue or a makeover. First it was Cinderella, then Sleeping Beauty was all anyone could talk about, next Snow White came onto the scene, and now it's some girl named Rapunzel's turn in the spotlight. I can barely keep track of them! You'd think the Charming brothers were in a competition to find and marry the neediest woman.

By the way, who is naming these people? *Snow*

White is not a name, that's a description! *Cinderella* is just cruel and *Rapunzel* sounds like something that happens to fruit when it's left in the sun. Do famous people name their kids ridiculous things just to tick off the rest of us?

It's not just the damsels in distress that are all the rage. Have you noticed every village idiot with a quirk becomes national news? Jack and Jill fell down a hill—*so what?* Little Bo Peep lost her sheep—*how is that my problem?* Hickory, dickory, dock, the mouse ran up the clock—*call pest control, not me!*

We're inherently teaching our children that the bigger a numbskull you are, the more attention you'll get. In my day, it was the *knights in shining armor* and the *valiant leaders* who got the respect. You actually had to do something significant to earn notoriety. Just because times are simpler now doesn't mean we should celebrate every moron under the sun!

The Fairy Godmother tells us we've entered a "Golden Age." I say we've entered a "snooze fest." Everything is so peaceful and happy it's driving me

nuts. Too much smiling can't be good for the soul. And if I hear one more schmuck say the phrase *happily ever after* I'm going to beat them with the heel of my buckled shoe. Who came up with *that*? And why do we have to say it at the end of *everything*?

The phrase was so catchy, the Fairy Godmother established the *Happily Ever After Assembly* with the Fairy Council and the current kings and queens of the kingdoms. I wanted nothing to do with it, but she insisted I join. Now I'm expected to contribute to the *progress* and *prosperity* of our world, when I'd rather just mock it from afar.

I'm not sure why she wanted me around, but I

owe the Fairy Godmother one. I've felt terrible ever since I turned down the chance to be her apprentice. I've never met someone who cares so genuinely about making life better for the people and creatures in our world than the Fairy Godmother—I could never fill her shoes!

The Fairy Godmother's a great gal and an excellent friend. We've been close since we were kids. We're always there for each other, through thick and thin. I held her hand when she gave birth to both of her sons, and provided a shoulder to cry on when her husband died. In return, she's always posted my bail and testified as a character witness—*you don't get closer than that!*

The Fairy Godmother has always seen something in me that no one, including myself, has seen before. Despite all my mistakes and bad habits that the other fairies are so quick to berate me for, the Fairy Godmother defends me and has my back. She says I bring a lot of good into the world, whether I believe it or not. I just hope I never disappoint her.

Once again, she was the only person who remembered

it was my two hundredth birthday today. She made a huge obnoxious cake like she does every year. There were so many candles, it almost set the Fairy Palace on fire. I suppose it's sweet of her, but no woman wants to be reminded they're two centuries old. Maybe that's why I woke up so grumpy?

Well, I've got to do something before my bad mood becomes permanent. I just need a change of pace, a change of scenery, and definitely a change of people! Unfortunately, that isn't likely to happen anytime soon. I better find something to do with my time or I'm going to be in trouble.

Maybe I'll start up a hobby. Does ale tasting or gambling count? I want to start with something I'm good at.

5 GA (Golden Age)

Dear Diary,

Well, gambling didn't help matters. Now on top of being annoyed by everyone around me, I owe most of them money, too. I've lost practically all the earnings from my wrestling days. I tried to start a comeback by wrestling unicorns, but it didn't have the same draw that the dragons had. No one wants to pay admission to see an old lady put a snooty horse in a headlock.

I did manage to score *one* good win in a card game last week—*a golden egg!* Now, as everyone knows, golden eggs are usually made of solid gold.

But if you're lucky, it'll be fertilized! Which means a magic goose will hatch that *lays* golden eggs!

As luck would have it, on my way home from the card game I felt something moving inside the egg! *It was definitely fertilized!* I was going to be rich! I'd never have to worry about gambling debts again! Finally, after helping so many idiots achieve a happily-ever-after, I was going to get my own!

I was terribly paranoid that something would happen to the little zygote, so I made it as comfortable as possible until it was ready to hatch. I carefully wrapped it in blankets and rested it by the fireplace to stay warm. I even cradled it and sang soothing songs to it. (Actually, I don't have a good singing voice, so it probably thought it was on a sinking ship.)

Eventually, the little chick started pecking at the shell. *This was it!* With every piece it chucked away I thought of another extravagant purchase I was going to make with its future eggs. A beach house in Mermaid Bay, a country estate in the Charming Kingdom, a cabin in the Dwarf Forests—the possibilities were endless!

Unfortunately, wealth wasn't in my immediate future after all. A *gander* hatched out of the egg! That's right—*a useless male goose!* I could kiss my expensive dreams good-bye.

I thought I was disappointed to see him, but you should have seen the look he gave me! The goose looked me up and down and shook his head judgmentally. He squawked at me, and although I'm not as fluent in bird as I am in other animal dialects, I could have sworn he said, "No, this isn't right. You can't possibly be my mother."

"You think *you're* disappointed? You were supposed to be my retirement fund! Now what am I supposed to do with you?" I said.

The gander eyed my stomach and squawked again, as if to say, *"Judging by your midsection, I'm afraid to ask."*

"I'm not going to *eat you*, smart aleck," I said. "You look far too gamey for my taste. I might get the runs just from looking at you!"

His beak dropped open as if it was the most offensive thing he had ever heard—and I had to remind myself that it probably was, since he was only a minute old.

He squawked again and headed for the door as if to say, *"I just hatched out of a golden egg! I will not put up with this treatment."*

"Don't let the door hit your tail feathers on the way out!" I yelled after him. "Good luck lasting outside! There are plenty of hungry creatures in the woods that would *love* a gamey snack!"

The gander slammed the door and left my house. He was surprisingly strong for an infant. I didn't let it upset me, though. It takes more than a feathered tantrum to grind my gears.

I poured myself a glass of bubbly and cozied up in my favorite rocking chair. I was looking forward to a nice quiet night alone, but I couldn't stop thinking about the little guy.

What had I done? He wasn't even an hour old yet and I let him waddle into a forest with no protection. I couldn't just sit there—I had to find him! I just hoped it wasn't too late.

I ran outside into the woods with a lantern raised

above my head. Thank-
fully, it had snowed the
night before, so I was
able to follow his tiny
webbed footprints into
the forest. I found the
little bugger standing
in a clearing in the
middle of the woods.
Thankfully, he was
alive . . . *but he wasn't
alone!*

A giant wolf with matted black fur and red eyes
was walking in circles around him. The poor goose
was trembling and, from the way he covered the
nostrils on his beak, I'm assuming the wolf had
terrible breath.

"Poor, poor little birdy," the wolf said. "All alone
in the woods without a father or mother goose to
protect him. Do you know what happens to little
goslings when they're all by themselves?"

The wolf grinned, exposing his sharp, pointy

teeth. The little gander squawked, as if to say, *"I seriously regret asking you for directions."*

"Hey! Get away from him!" I demanded.

"Who are you?" the wolf asked.

"Consider me the *mother goose*!" I said. "And I don't like the way you're taunting my kid."

"Your *kid*?" the wolf laughed, not intimidated by me in the slightest. "Silly old woman! Go knit something before you become dessert."

Knit something? Old woman? Clearly this mutt had a death wish.

"I'm not the knitting type, *pup*," I said and pulled up my sleeve to show him my forearm. "Do you see this scar? I got it from wrestling a dragon three times your size—and that was for *fun!* So unless you want me to knock all the teeth out of your ugly muzzle, I suggest you find a nice fruit salad to prey on and leave my goose alone!"

The wolf growled at me and then ran into the trees, leaving the gander and me alone for good. The gander sighed with relief and there was a thankful twinkle in his eyes. He waddled up to my feet and squawked at me, as if to say, "Mother Goose, *huh?*"

I never would have considered myself the maternal type, but it did have a nice ring to it. I figured if I was going to adopt, I'd better do it in my early two hundreds while I was still vital. Besides, the goose's options were limited.

"I'm probably the best mother you're going to get around here. I doubt anything else is going to tolerate you long enough to take care of you."

The gander shrugged. Even he couldn't deny he was a pain in the backside.

"So what are we going to call *you*, mister?"

He squawked again. *"What about* Enrique Rodriguez?*"*

"I like *Lester*," I said. "I promised an old tavern buddy I would name my firstborn after him. I think you're the closest thing I'll ever get to that."

The gander rolled his eyes and sighed. "Fine," he squawked. *"Lester* it is—can we go inside now? No one told me outside was going to be so cold."

Over the last week, Lester and I have gotten to

know each other and are slowly getting used to living together. We've had all the conversations new roommates typically have, like *Don't leave your feathers in the sink, No regurgitating at the table,* and *The floor is not a toilet* (he's not the first roommate I've had these conversations with, but that's a long story). It's been challenging, but I think we'll iron out all the kinks in time.

Mother Goose has really grown on me, too. Everyone on the Happily Ever After Assembly thinks it's adorable that I'm taking care of Lester, so my new nickname is the only thing they address me by anymore.

It's a good thing, too, because with all my recent gambling debts, I needed a new name....

7 GA

Dear Diary,

Things haven't been great between Lester and me lately. We're constantly arguing about how he needs to do something with his life, but there's not an ounce of ambition in his hollow bones. All he does is sit at home and eat junk food all day while I'm at work. He's gotten so fat he's practically the size of a horse. So, I decided to *use him like a horse!*

For years, my main method of transportation has been magical teleportation, and I've never been good at it. I always end up inside a wall or a cabinet— especially when I have a hangover. So, one afternoon I brought home reins and a saddle and strapped up m'gander! I was going to make use of him if it killed me.

Lester wasn't thrilled by the idea. He had one look at himself in the mirror and shook his head. "You've got to be kidding me," he squawked.

"Come on, let's do a test flight before the winds change!"

Our first takeoff was pretty easy. Lester insisted he needed a running start with my added weight, but I think he was being difficult on purpose. Turns out Lester is a decent flyer, although I would never tell him that because it would go straight to his head. He didn't take directions well, so I just jerked on the reins until he listened. I'm surprised they didn't break off.

Believe it or not, Lester's not the first winged creature I've piloted. During the Dragon Age, I used to fly a dragon named Schnapps. Boy was he ugly! He had the face of a boar, wings like a bat, the body of a salamander, and the temper of a wet cat. I had to give him up after he ate one of my coworkers—you know, workplace politics.

I had forgotten how wonderful it felt to fly. The best part of riding Lester was that everyone looking up from below just thought he was a regular bird in the sky. They had no idea this wacky old lady was riding on his back. This will be useful the next time a bounty hunter is tailing me.

Landing was not Lester's strong suit. After our first flight, he hit the ground so hard I was thrown off his back and somersaulted through a muddy strip of land. I think it was calculated on his part. I've never heard a goose laugh so hard.

Our second landing was even worse! We crashed into the roof of a schoolhouse, terrifying and emotionally scarring two dozen schoolchildren. It was a mess! There were feathers and pencils everywhere. I've been getting nasty letters from their parents all week. I'm sure we'll get blamed for every issue their children have in the future.

We've had a rocky start, but we'll get the hang of it!

Dear Diary,

*W*hat *a day!* I thought Humpty Dumpty's death was going to be the biggest shock of my year, but boy was I wrong. The Fairy Council and I finally found out why the Fairy Godmother has been acting so strange lately—*and it's a doozy!*

It all started when she called an impromptu assembly meeting at the Fairy Palace. I begrudgingly got out of bed and dragged Lester out of his, and off we went. We flew to the palace, landed on the mattress the fairies placed in the garden for us, and met the other fairies in the great hall.

Usually she only calls us there when something

wonderful has happened we all need to know about, so I wasn't exactly thrilled to be there.

"Well, what is it this time?" I asked them. "Let me guess, Suzie Daffodil was rescued from a tower by Prince Bright Teeth? Or did Johnnie Alibi finally find his herd of scapegoats?"

"We don't know," Emerelda said. "We're still waiting for the Fairy Godmother to arrive."

That wasn't a surprise. The Fairy Godmother had been late or absent to all the assembly meetings that month. On the rare occasions we saw her, she always came in a huff and left in a hurry. Like I said, we knew something was wrong, but no one could get ahold of her long enough to ask what was going on.

A quick gust of sparkling wind blew into the great hall and the Fairy Godmother appeared. She always arrives in style, I'll give her that.

"Sorry I'm late!" she apologized. "I hope I didn't keep you waiting long."

Her cheeks were rosy and she was out of breath. She looked exactly like she used to after a long night of dancing when we were teenagers.

"Is everything all right, Fairy Godmother?" Xanthous asked. "You seem a little . . . *distressed*."

"Well, *distressed* isn't the word I would use," she said. "I have something I need to tell you. It'll be hard to believe at first, but it'll explain why I haven't been myself lately."

"I know what it is," I said with a sly grin. "You got a *boyfriend*!"

"What?" everyone said in unison, as if I had said something offensive.

"Oh, come on," I said. "She's *old*, not dead! Lots of men are dating older women these days. Besides, this is exactly how she acted when she met her late husband."

"Um . . . *no*, Mother Goose," the Fairy Godmother said. "I don't have a boyfriend."

"It's okay, FG," I said, trying to coax it out of her. "No one here is going to judge you! Your husband has been dead for years—it's perfectly acceptable to move on. Just tell us who he is! Is it King White? The Shoemaker? *The Traveling Tradesman?* Like I said, no judgments!"

It was obvious from the look she was giving me that a boyfriend hadn't been distracting her. It was something else entirely of a very serious nature. What a shame; I was hoping her boyfriend would have a friend.

"I've discovered another dimension," the Fairy Godmother blurted out.

Everyone in the room gasped. Lester let out a prolonged squawk. I started laughing but quickly stopped when I realized she wasn't joking.

"Another dimension?" Skylene asked.

"You must be joking!" Tangerina said.

"How is that possible?" Rosette said.

"I don't know, but I assure you it's real," the Fairy Godmother said.

At first, I was convinced she was hitting the pixie dust. She couldn't have actually discovered another dimension! That's crazier than a chicken with its feet glued to the ground! But being *late* and *absent* was one thing; *exaggerating the truth* was something the Fairy Godmother never did.

"How did you discover it?" Emerelda asked.

"Well . . . it was shortly after Cinderella's

wedding," the Fairy Godmother explained. "After seeing how much a little magic changed her life, I was inspired to help people more than ever. So, I decided to cast a spell that would take me to whomever needed magic the most. I waved my wand over my body, and the next thing I knew, I was someplace no one from our world had ever been before."

"What's it like?" Violetta asked.

"Horrible," she said. "Just like the Dragon Age, only the destruction is caused by man. It's a world of vastly different cultures in vastly different terrains, all fighting one another for dominance."

"Were you scared?" Coral asked.

"I was horrified," she said, "but not as frightened as a little boy I found hiding in the rubble. He was trembling and starving. Barbarians had destroyed his village and killed his family. I gave him some food and took him to safety. However, the only thing that lifted his spirits was when I told him the stories of Cinderella and Rapunzel."

I couldn't help rolling my eyes at the sound of their ridiculous names.

"Why did that cheer him up?" Xanthous asked.

"Because in the other dimension, or the *Otherworld* as I call it, there is no magic," the Fairy Godmother said. "Hearing how magic helped and influenced the people in our world let the poor boy forget his troubles for just a moment. It brought him a little peace during the worst time of his life."

"Is the little boy all right now?" Coral asked.

"Yes—but that's the strangest thing about the Otherworld," the Fairy Godmother said. "I found an elderly couple who agreed to look after the boy so I could return to this world. I was only here a week or so, but by the time I returned to the Otherworld to check on him, the boy had become a *man*! He had a wife and children of his own."

"A man?" Tangerina said. "Do they grow faster in the other dimension?"

"The Otherworld moves much faster than our world does," she said. "A day for us may be months to them. A year could be a century."

"Remarkable!" Skylene said.

"The man said my stories saved his life and they

gave him hope after a devastating time. He passed them down to his own children and called them *fairy tales.* I've been returning to the Otherworld every chance I get to spread our stories to other children in need."

"That explains your recent behavior," Emerelda said.

"I apologize for my negligence," the Fairy Godmother said. "Every time I travel to the Otherworld it's in much worse shape than the time before. There are more and more children who desperately need something to believe in. Which brings me to the reason I asked you to meet me today. I've seen firsthand what a difference these stories have made in the children's lives, but I can't continue doing it alone. The more of us there are, the more likely I think the stories have a chance of being heard. So, I'm hopeful you all will join me in spreading the stories of our world around the Otherworld."

The great hall became very quiet, like when a friend who owes you money asks for more. It was so tense, I openly took a swig from the flask I hide in my bonnet—I didn't even try to sneak it.

"Show us this world," Xanthous said. "How can we get there?"

"The magic of traveling between worlds is so unique, I believe I'm the only one capable of it," the Fairy Godmother said. "But I've managed to put that magic into a portal. Follow me, I'll show you where it is."

The Fairy Godmother led us to the south tower of the Fairy Palace. The room was circular and empty except for an archway that had been built in the center. The Fairy Godmother pulled a lever on the wall and a blue curtain appeared under the arch. Beyond the curtain was a very bright room.

"This is one of many portals I plan on creating if you agree to help me," she said. "The Otherworld is just through this curtain—but brace yourselves, the journey may be a shock."

She stepped through the curtain, and we followed her. I told Lester to stay behind—he gets gassy when he's overwhelmed.

I was wrong about the other side of the curtain;
it wasn't a room of light, but a *world of light*! For a
moment I thought I was the one on pixie dust! We
fell through a bright, never-ending space for what
felt like forever. I saw the other fairies spinning and
circling around me. There didn't seem to be an end
in sight until all nine of us landed in a damp grassy
field.

I got up and looked around at the Otherworld
with my own eyes. It was even worse than the Fairy
Godmother described.

"What a dump!" I said.

At first, I thought an amazing party had
happened the night before, because there were
hundreds of passed-out men scattered around the
field. The fairies screamed when they saw the men.
I took a closer look and realized the bodies weren't
unconscious but *dead*! A terrible battle had happened
here, not a party. And if the smell was any indication,
it had happened a while ago.

"What a terrible place," Tangerina said.

"I've never seen such a sad sight," Violetta sniffed.

"This isn't even the worst I've seen," the Fairy Godmother said. "Women and children are also slaughtered in times of war. Mercy is a very rare privilege in this world."

In the distance, there were people taking the armor, the weapons, and any goods they could find off the bodies. Tears came to the fairies' eyes. If I were in touch with my emotions, mine would have welled up, too.

The Fairy Godmother led us to the closest village, and our spirits sank even more. There was poverty everywhere you looked. With no homes to go to, mothers sat on the side of the road cradling their crying infants. Children begged for food and money from everyone they saw. We gave them everything we had—although none of them wanted my bonnet, which was a little offensive. Apparently beggars *can* be choosers.

"Do you understand why I'm so passionate about helping the people here?" the Fairy Godmother asked. "We've made our world a safe and peaceful place, and now I believe magic has brought us here to do the same. Will you help me help them?"

The fairies looked at one another in a very determined manner.

"I will," Emerelda said.

"As will I," Xanthous said.

"Absolutely," Skylene and Tangerina said together.

"You can count on us," Violetta said, and Coral nodded.

"With you one hundred percent," Rosette said.

Everyone turned to me because I was the only one who hadn't agreed to it yet. I hesitated because I was scared. I could barely help the people in our world. How was I going to make a difference in a place like this?

"And what about you, Mother Goose?" the Fairy Godmother asked.

"Okay, I'll join, too," I said. "I just hope I don't make things worse."

Lesson learned: *Be careful what you wish for.* When I hoped for a place to escape to now and then, I never thought I'd end up in the likes of the Otherworld. What have I gotten myself into?

1349, London (Otherworld)

Dear Diary,

Today was my first solo trip into the Otherworld, and, boy, was I dreading it. For months I've been listening to the fairies brag about all the children they've been helping and it's intimidated my socks off. Their stories are so touching and heartfelt, I knew I could never have the same impact.

For starters, the fairies really look the part. They're always dressed in bright, shimmering, colorful clothes, like they're performing in an obnoxious parade. I get headaches if I look at them for too long, and children love that gimmicky crap.

Another thing: I've never been good with kids. They never appreciate my humor. They say I talk funny and smell weird, which stings when it's coming from a kid with a lisp who's covered in chocolate. Every baby I've ever been in contact with has peed or thrown up on me—even when I'm not holding it! It's like I'm a walking hazardous wastebasket to them.

Needless to say, I was very nervous about the whole thing. I seriously regretted signing up for it.

I crossed through the portal and ended up in a town called London in a country called England. I've heard the fairies speak so highly of it, but it was miserable! Or at least the condition I found it in was.

The city was like a big foggy maze, and there were rats everywhere! The streets were filled with people lying on the ground who coughed and moaned horribly—like I do on the mornings after I've had too much bubbly. But these people weren't recovering from a night of careless drinking, they were *sick*—the sickest I've ever seen!

Their skin was pale and there were dark circles under their eyes. Their glands were so swollen they protruded out of their necks and down their bodies. Their fingers and toes were black, as if their bodies had begun rotting while they were still alive.

I use the term *alive* loosely, because many looked like they were already dead. I couldn't help but scream when I turned a corner and found a large pile of bodies stacked right in the middle of town. The liveliest person I saw was a man wearing a birdlike mask who was pulling a wagon of more dead bodies, which he dumped with the others.

"Excuse me, sir." I said. "I'm new in town. What's going on here?"

"Madame, you mustn't be walking the streets without a mask on!" he said. "You'll catch the *Black Death*."

"Black Death?" I asked. "Where I come from, that's a wrestling move I invented. What does it mean here?"

"It's a terrible plague," he said. "It's taken more

than half the lives in this country, and even more throughout Europe."

"*A plague?*" I said in disbelief.

Of course! There *would* be a deadly epidemic the first time I came to the Otherworld by myself—it was just my luck. How was I supposed to help anyone under these circumstances? If I wasn't nervous before, I definitely was now. I needed a drink.

"Is there a tavern around here?" I asked him.

"What's a tavern?" he asked.

"You know, a place that serves alcoholic beverages," I explained, but that didn't register with him, either.

"Alcohol?" he asked.

"Yeah, the sterilizing liquid originally invented for medicinal purposes but was later developed into a variety of consumable flavors for consumers to abuse."

Still, it wasn't ringing a bell.

"I've never heard of a *tavern*, but it's a fine idea," the man said.

"Never mind," I said. "Do you know of any children in the area who could use a hand?"

He pointed down a winding street. "There's a church down this road that's housing orphans, but I wouldn't go there if I were you. All the children are infected."

"Trust me, it'll take more than a plague to poison the blood in my veins," I said. "Thank you for the directions."

I traveled down the road and stopped at a building that had several tiny coffins stacked outside it. I figured this must be the place. It was an eerie sight, and my heart began to race. Thankfully I found my backup flask in my hat and took a swig from it.

I knocked on the door and a nun wearing a mask answered. I could only see her eyes, but the dark circles under them were just as bad as the people's outside. However, hers weren't from illness but exhaustion.

"Can I help you?" she asked me.

"I was wondering if I could help *you*," I said. "I was in the neighborhood and thought I'd ask if you needed any assistance with the children."

"God bless you," the nun said. She was so relieved I thought she might kiss me. "I've been taking care of the orphans for two days straight without sleep. Please come in."

The nun led me inside the church and took me into a back room. There were a dozen beds but only three were occupied with children: two boys and one girl. They had terrible coughs and were just as pale and swollen as the people outside. One of the boys was so ill he could barely keep his eyes open.

"The plague took their parents," the nun said. "A week ago we were turning children away, and now these are who remain...."

"Why don't you get some rest," I said. "I'll look after the kiddos."

"Thank you," the nun said and went into the next room. She was so weary, she didn't even think to ask who I was or if I was qualified to look after children. The orphans, however, weren't so shy about vetting me.

"Who are you?" the conscious little boy wheezed.

"Where I'm from, they call me Mother Goose," I said.

"Do you have children?" he asked.

"Nope," I said. "But I do have a pet gander who acts like a child—though don't tell him I said that. He'll get very upset."

"Geese don't get upset," the little girl said.

"You've never met Lester," I told her.

"He has a name?" the boy asked.

"Sure does, although he tells me every day he wants to change it to something more dignified."

"He can *talk*?" the girl asked.

"Getting him to shut up is the trick," I said.

"But animals can't talk," the boy said.

"Where I'm from, lots of animals talk," I said. "They wear clothes, have jobs, and are respectable members of society. We have lots of things you don't have in this world, because in my world there's lots of magic."

"Magic?" the girl asked, as if she was afraid of it. "Do you work for the *devil*?"

"Depends on who you ask," I said. "But you have nothing to worry about. I work for the Fairy Godmother. She's a wonderful woman who sent me here to help you."

The orphans began to cough and looked at each other sadly.

"You can't help us," the boy said. "No one can. Soon the Lord will take us to be with our parents."

I didn't know what to say to him. Who would?

"I may not be able to help your bodies, but maybe I can put your minds at ease," I said. "Would you like to hear a story?"

The orphans just looked at me. They didn't say no, so I figured this was my chance. I had no idea which story I was going to tell them. What could I possibly tell them to make them feel better? I anxiously took another swig from my flask and began telling them the first tale that came to mind.

"*Humpty Dumpty sat on a wall, Humpty Dumpty had a great fall; all the king's horses and all the king's men couldn't put Humpty back together again,*" I said and hiccupped.

"Why are you rhyming?" the girl asked.

"Oh no, was I rhyming?" I asked—I hadn't even noticed. "You'll have to forgive me. I tend to rhyme when I've had too much to drink. It's a nasty trait I get from my father—it runs in the family."

"I like it," the boy said and smiled, probably for the first time in a long while. "My parents used to tell me rhymes before they died."

They seemed like such sweet kids. I didn't think there was anything I could say to comfort them.

"You know, I was an orphan, too, once," I said. "My dad was a warlock and my mom was a fairy. They had me very young, probably before they wanted to. They left me on the doorstep of the Fairy Palace and ran off to persue their dreams of becoming musicians. But their musical aspirations were crushed when a giant stepped on them."

"That's rough," the girl said.

"It could have been worse," I said. "The fairies raised me, but I was a bit of a troublemaker. I got passed around from home to home until I could take care of myself. I was always using my magic to play pranks and rig horse races."

It was the first time I had ever told anyone that story, and I had told it to the right audience. Both orphans were smiling at me.

"I'm sorry you lost your parents," the boy said.

"Me too," I said. "You'd think people with their heads in the clouds would have seen a big foot coming."

Wouldn't you know it—*I made them laugh!* It was the most heartwarming sound I've ever heard. It reminded me that I had a heart, and judging from the warmth filling my chest, I must have had a big one.

"Mother Goose?"

I turned my head and saw that the other little boy

was now wide-awake and sitting up in bed, as if their laughter had brought him back to life.

"Will you tell us another story?" he said. "Rhymes make me happy."

After hearing this, I realized my tear ducts still worked after all. I took another big swig from my flask and told them another story.

"Little Bo Peep has lost her sheep, and doesn't know where to find them; leave them alone, and they'll come home, wagging their tails behind them."

"We used to have a farm with sheep before the plague," the girl said. "Please tell us another one."

"Little Miss Muffet sat on a tuffet, eating her curds and whey; along came a spider, who sat down beside her, and frightened Miss Muffet away."

"A spider?" the boys laughed together. "Please don't stop!"

"Jack and Jill went up a hill to fetch a pail of water; Jack fell down and broke his crown, and Jill came tumbling after."

I spent the rest of the night telling them rhymes about the ridiculous people from my world. I had sobered up entirely but kept a loose facade to keep them happy. They had me repeat their favorites, and then we recited them together. The orphans added tunes to the poems and we sang them to one another until they began to fall asleep.

"Mother Goose, will you be here in the morning?" the girl asked.

"You betcha," I said. "Now you kiddos get a good night's sleep, and we'll rhyme more in the morning."

I sat with them until the sun rose, but the orphans never woke up. Just like the boy said, the Lord took them to be with their parents. When she was done resting, the nun came into the room, said a prayer for their souls, and covered their bodies with their bed sheets.

Naturally, a part of me was devastated. But knowing I managed to supply those kids with a little happiness in their final moments was the best feeling I've ever felt, and perhaps the single greatest act I've ever done. For the first time, I truly understood why the Fairy Godmother was so passionate about helping people. There's nothing like restoring the light in someone's eyes and helping them forget their pain, even if it's just for a moment. It's magic at its finest.

I went into the Otherworld hoping to make a difference in someone's life, but the true difference was made in mine. I had been so skeptical of myself before, but making those orphans laugh in such a miserable time had a profound effect on me. Maybe this old lady *could* help that world after all. . . .

1428, France

Dear Diary,

Today, I was back in Europe spreading stories and rhymes around France. What a mess this war between the English and French has been! Every time I return to the Otherworld *it's still going on*. I swear it's lasted at least a hundred years.

There's so much commotion in the streets, you can barely hear your own thoughts. I needed a quiet place to rest, but that almost seemed impossible to find with all the soldiers running amok. I passed a cathedral just on the edge of town and decided it was probably my best bet.

I was right; the cathedral was heavenly inside.

It was so quiet, you could hear a feather float! There wasn't a soul in sight—except for the paintings and statues of all the Catholic saints, obviously. I lay down on the first pew I found and had a quick snooze.

I was having a wonderful dream about mud-wrestling ogres in a massive sold-out arena when something awoke me. A teenage girl was kneeling in the center of the cathedral, obnoxiously praying aloud. Although my French isn't as good as my German, I could make out what she was saying.

"Please, Lord, send me a sign like you did when I was a child," she pleaded. "Tell me how to recover France from the English and put Charles VII on the throne."

Are all teenagers incapable of having internal thoughts? Can't they have feelings without letting the whole world know about them? When I was a teenage girl, I always kept to myself. Granted, I was in a witness protection program, but that's a story for another time.

What this girl should have prayed for was new

clothes and decent soap. She was filthy, she wore boys' clothes, and her hair was more tangled than a rat's nest—total tomboy. She wasn't going to get Charlie's attention looking like a pig wrangler.

It took me a minute to realize she must have been that local loon everyone was always talking about in the taverns—which, by the way, are *everywhere* now! You're welcome, Europe!

They said she's super-pushy and entitled and annoys the heck out of everyone in town. That sounds like *every* teenager where I'm from; I don't know why they're making her so significant. The people in this world are weird about whom they do and don't talk about.

Her name is Joan something—was it *Joan of Snark?* Or maybe it was *Arc?* Well, whoever she was, she was seriously getting on my nerves. I had to get her out of there so she'd stop disturbing my nap.

"Please, heavenly Father," Joan prayed. "I am your humble servant. Give me guidance so I may satisfy your will!"

"*Jooooaaaan, JOOOOAAAAN!*" I moaned dramatically.

Joan rose excitedly and looked around the cathedral. "Is that you, Lord?" she asked desperately.

"*NOOOO,*" I said. After all, pretending to be God in his own house was just plain rude.

"Saint Margaret?" Joan asked. "Have *you* come to bless me with some guidance?"

"*YEEESSS! 'TIS I, SAINT MARGARET!*" I moaned.

"Oh, Saint Margaret!" Joan said and clutched her hands over her heart. "Thank you! Your wish is my command!"

"*THANK YOU, MY CHILD. I KNOW I CAN ALWAYS COUNT ON YOU. OUT OF EVERYONE FROM ARC, YOU ARE MY FAVORITE. NOW, YOU MUST RAISE AN ARMY AND DEFEND FRANCE, JOAN!*"

"Of course, Saint Margaret!"

"*LIBERATE FRANCE FROM THE ENGLISH!*"

"Whatever you say, Saint Margret!"

"HELP GOD PLACE CHARLES VII ON THE THRONE!"

"Oh yes, Saint Margret!"

"BUT WHATEVER YOU DO, JOAN..."

"What is it, Saint Margret? Please, tell me!"

"YOU MUST LEAVE THIS CATHEDRAL AT ONCE AND LOCK THE DOOR ON YOUR WAY OUT!"

"Anything you want, Saint Margaret!" Joan said. She leaped to her feet and ran out the door like a horse out of a burning barn.

I had a good long laugh to myself and then finished my nap. Poor Joan. I almost felt bad for misleading her. Clearly she wasn't the sharpest knife in the drawer. She'll be all right, though—hormones bring out the worst in every teenager.

1503, ITALY

Dear Diary,

I never thought these words would come from my
mouth—but I'm *in love*! His name is Leonardo
da Vinci, but I call him *Leo* for short. He's a painter,
sculptor, musician, mathematician, architect,
engineer, inventor, and writer! He's what they call a
Renaissance man!

I have to say, of all the trends I've started around
Europe, I'm most proud of the Renaissance. Without
it, someone like Leo may not have had the chance to
show off his talents. He probably would have been
burned at the stake, just like all the people in this
world who think outside the box.

I was getting so tired of all that medieval craziness—it was all *pillage this* and *torture that*. It got old really fast, so I finally said, "Come on, guys, let's spice some things up around here. Let's create some new philosophies! Cook some decent food! Hang some drapes! Learn to *enjoy* life a little bit!"

They really took my suggestions to heart, because the Renaissance was in full force by the time I came back to the Otherworld. Every day they built better buildings, created better music and art, and discovered advances in science and medicine! And of course, the man leading the world into this new era was none other than my Leo.

We first met in a tavern—even those had improved! He bought me a drink and said, "I'd give my left arm to paint a beautiful woman like you."

He was so charming, I melted on the spot. "Save your arm and just treat me to dinner," I said.

Leo took me to his favorite spot in Florence and we hit it off right away. We had so many similar interests—which wasn't a surprise, because Leo was

interested in *everything*. We had so much in common,
too. He also had a rocky childhood and knew what it
was like to be ahead of the world he lived in. He was
fascinated with my stories of the fairy-tale world and

thought what the fairies and I were doing was very noble.

Leo is more than one hundred and fifty years younger than me, so I felt a little insecure. But we were so intellectually in sync, you'd never know there was that big an age difference.

On our second date, Leo invited me to his place and painted my portrait. It was so difficult to sit still because he kept making me laugh. When he was finished, he claimed it would one day be known as his masterpiece.

"I'll call it the *Mona Goosa*," he said.

"Oh, don't name it that," I said. "Just in case a warlord comes looking for me, I wouldn't want you to get involved—it's a long story."

"Then how about the *Mona Lisa*?" he asked.

"Beautiful!" I told him. It takes a real gentleman to be so sensitive to a lady's needs.

The next time I went into the Otherworld, I brought Lester with me so he could meet Leo. Lester wasn't as taken with him as I was, but geese can be so territorial. Truth be told, I think Lester was a little jealous there was someone else in my life.

Leo loves going on flights with Lester and me. He enjoys it so much, he started sketching plans to build a *flying machine* so Lester doesn't have to carry both of us on his back. Lester really appreciated this, and I think Leo won him over.

I know I've been making fun of those *happily ever after* idiots back home for years, but that's because I've never felt like *this* before. Now I get why everyone is so smiley all the darn time. Leo makes me feel so complete, protected, and unstoppable—like I could take on the whole world if I had to! And if I don't stop gambling with warlords, I just might have to!

Who knows, there just might be a *Father Goose* in Lester's future.

1519, ITALY

Dear Diary,

I'm not going to lie, today is a sad day. Forbidding the trolls and goblins to leave their territory in the fairy-tale world has been keeping the fairies and me from traveling to the Otherworld as regularly. By the time I returned, Leo had passed away.

I don't know how I let it happen. I've always been aware of the time difference between worlds—I guess I just forgot. But that's love for you. It makes you careless and forgetful. It fools you into thinking the people you hold dear will be around forever, so you take them for granted.

I'm used to losing friends—that's what happens

when you live as long as I have—but losing Leo stings worse than anything I've felt before. I don't think I'll ever find someone like my Renaissance man again. . . .

1532, London

Dear Diary,

Well, I've met someone! He's smart, tall, likes food, enjoys jousting, and comes from a good family. Okay, I'll just say it—*he's King Henry VIII of England!*

I know, I know—England is still recovering from his messy separation from Catherine of Aragon. Can you believe Henry is going to separate England from the Roman Catholic Church just to get rid of her? She must have been terrible! And have you met the daughter, Mary? Good luck marrying her off!

All my friends have warned me that Henry probably isn't the best choice for a husband. He's

got major commitment phobia, he's always on the
verge of bankrupting the country, he's got a bad
temper, and he has more mistresses than he knows

what to do with. But really, who doesn't have baggage?

Lester can't stand Henry. He says the king is just a "rebound" after losing Leo. The goose might have a point; not a day goes by that I don't miss Leo terribly. Luckily, the wedding plans have been a good distraction from that.

Of course, when you're marrying into royalty, you're bound to run into a little controversy. There have been a lot of rumors circulating court that Henry has a thing for my good friend, Anne Boleyn. I've assured everyone their relationship is completely platonic! The reason Anne is around so much is because she's actually going to be one of my maids of honor; she'd never betray me by seducing my future husband!

Gosh, all of Henry's friends are so judgmental. I suppose that's why they call it *court*! Now I better get back to planning the big day. There's nothing like planning a party with an unlimited budget!

1565, London

Dear Diary,

Can you believe that backstabbing double-crosser Anne Boleyn? She stole my fiancé from me on the eve of our wedding and then had the nerve to name *me* as the godmother of their daughter, Elizabeth. It's all right, though; Anne got what she deserved in the end. People are still talking about that amazing party I threw on the night of her execution.

Regardless of her terrible parents, I ended up growing a soft spot for Elizabeth. She was such an intelligent, strong, and feisty child—she reminded me a lot of myself when I was her age. I knew the pressures of being a Tudor woman in a Tudor man's

world, so I looked out for her when she was growing up.

Even though she was third in line for the throne, I always had a feeling Elizabeth would be queen one day. And thankfully for England, I was right.

I was in the London area telling some peasant children fairy tales, so she invited me over for brunch. I could tell she was a little stressed because her ruff was extra thick today.

"Liz, what's wrong?" I asked.

"My advisors keep telling me I need to marry and provide an heir to the throne," she said. "They say my position as queen won't be secure until I do so."

"That's a load of goose droppings!" I said. "You're the best monarch this country has had since William the Conqueror."

"It's not that I'm against marriage or children," Elizabeth said. "But have you seen the options they've presented me with? And I thought *my* cousins were inbred!"

"Well, I may still be bitter and burned from everything I went through with your father, but I think marriage is the worst!" I said. "You've got a good thing going here, Lizzie. You don't want a man coming in here and messing it up for you."

"I suppose you're right," she said. "So, what am I to do? What should I tell my advisors?"

"Tell them you *are* married . . . *to England*!" I said. "Say you'll consider marriage when and only when they can find you a suitable, smart, and handsome prince with no political agenda. Until then, declare yourself *the Virgin Queen*! Say you're staying pure for God and for your people's best interests. You'll be a rock star!"

Elizabeth thought about it for a moment and then nodded her head—well, as much as that ruffled thing around her neck would allow.

"Now, enough virgin talk," I said. "Tell me what's been going on with you and Robert Dudley! Everyone knows he's got the hots for you!"

1590, JAPAN

Dear Diary,

I'm sorry I've been missing in action for a while, but I've got a good excuse. For the last five years, Lester and I have been living in a secret ninja clan deep in the Kii Mountains of Japan. I know I've said this before, but that was just because I had missed a bunch of Happily Ever After Assembly meetings and the Fairy Council was ticked off. This time the ninja were real and I have the battle scars to prove it.

It all started when we visited the secluded village of Koka to spread fairy tales to the children living there. Had I known the village was secretly a training camp for ninja warriors, I would have worn more comfortable pants. From the way I dressed, the ninja instantly assumed I was a samurai spy, which I took as a major compliment given my age. They captured us and threatened our lives.

Our only chance of survival was pledging our sole allegiance to their clan. Yeah, I probably could have whipped all their skinny butts with my eyes closed, but after everything I went through with Henry VIII, it felt good to join a club.

We spent the next several months learning all the ancient traditions and arts of ninjutsu. We had espionage Mondays, assassination Tuesdays, combat Wednesdays, deception Thursdays, and finger painting Fridays. I guess ninja are really into finger painting—who knew?

Once I mastered the skills taught to me, I began teaching the ninja a few of my famous wrestling moves from back in the day. They loved hearing my stories about dragons, so I gained a lot of respect. They called me *Kunoichi Okāsan*, which means *Mother Ninja*, and they called Lester *Debuna Yatsu*, which means *the fat one*.

We worked for the local landowners and used our skills against the corrupt samurai that were invading the land. These were some of the most intense battles of my life. Each time we went out on a job, not all of us returned.

I'm not proud of everything we did, but at least I made some major dough.

Eventually, the samurai caught up with us. A samurai warlord known as Oda Nobunaga, or *Cowabunga*, as I called him, invaded our area and wiped out all the ninja clans in the providence, including Koka. The survivors fled to the Kii

Mountains, and we've been here since. We spend each day plotting our revenge, but I think I'm beginning to lose interest.

It's been one heck of an experience—I never thought *ninja warrior* would be something I could add to my résumé—but I'm ready to go home. There are certain moments in your life when you look around and realize *you don't belong*, and this is one of those moments. It feels just like the time we joined Christopher Columbus's ship thinking it was a Mediterranean cruise.

I'm not sure Lester is cut out for a life of espionage anyway. All this ninjutsu seems to be going to his head. Lately, he's insisted I refer to him only as *the crane*. It'll be good for both of us to get out of this mountain air and get back to our day jobs.

1719, The Caribbean

Dear Diary,

S ometimes you just need a girls' weekend—or in my case, it was six months on the high seas aboard the pirate ship called *Revenge*. I was a cocaptain with my friends Anne Bonny and Mary Read, who I met in Jamaica a few years ago. We had all just gotten out of bad relationships and were looking for something spontaneous to do.

After a few rounds of drinks, we decided stealing a ship and setting sail around the Caribbean was exactly what we needed—and we were right! I'm glad they suggested it, because I was just going to recommend new haircuts.

There's nothing more healing after a breakup than pirating a ship full of men and bringing them to their knees. We stole our weight in gold and then buried it on exotic islands that only we knew existed.

We had some great times aboard that ship. We swore to one another we'd never return to shore and we'd live the rest of our lives on the water. Unfortunately, Anne's ex-boyfriend, the pirate John "Calico Jack" Rackham, eventually caught up to us (it was his ship after all). Naturally, he and Anne ended up getting back together, and our sisterhood was never the same.

Mary stayed with Anne and John, but I had to leave. I loved the ocean, but I needed to return to my normal dual-dimensional life. Believe it or not, I was starting to miss Lester and the fairies.

1774, Versailles

Dear Diary,

L ester and I were at the most amazing party last night at the *Palace of Versailles*! You know you've had a good time when you wake up on a chaise lounge floating in a fountain and have zero recollection of how you got there. That Marie Antoinette sure knows how to have a good time! It's so sweet of her to keep inviting me to her parties, despite her in-laws' opinions of me.

The French royals and I have never gotten along. It all started a century ago, when I accidently said, "Excuse me, ma'am" to Louis XIV. In my defense, the guy was wearing a long curly wig and high heels.

Anyone would have made that mistake. Since then I've been put on the *do not invite* list.

Marie has always had a hard time getting the French's approval, too; that's probably why we bonded so quickly when we met at that opera in Paris. They blame her for *everything*, just like the Fairy Council is always so quick to point their finger at me.

Anyhow, I swam my way out of the fountain, found my shoes and hat scattered in the garden (don't remember how that happened, either), and stumbled back inside the palace. Lester was still asleep on a couch inside; the gander would sleep through an asteroid hitting the earth if he was up too late the night before.

There was so much champagne and dessert left over from the night before; the maids were *still* cleaning it up. I wrapped up a couple of pieces of leftover cake to take home—there's no cake like Versailles cake!

I found Marie in her chambers. She had been up for hours and her hair was already perfectly in place and soared two feet above her head. *Now that's a party MVP!*

"Marie, I just wanted to thank you again for such a wonderful night!" I said. "I haven't had that much fun since the Crusades."

"Mother Goose! Thank God you're alive! After you fell out the window last night, we thought you were dead!" Marie said.

"Well, that explains the kink in my neck," I said. "From the looks of it, I must have continued the party in the gardens."

Suddenly, a soldier ran inside. He was sweating and out of breath, but we didn't think much of it at first. The Palace of Versailles is so big, everyone is usually sweating and out of breath by the time they got to Marie's room.

"*Madame, the palace is under attack! Hundreds of villagers are storming the gates! They say they're starving!*" the guard said.

"Oh no, what should we do?" Marie asked.

"May I make a suggestion?" I said. "You've got tons of food left over from the party. Why don't you offer them some cake? I'm sure they'll appreciate it—it was some of the best cake I've ever had!"

"That's a wonderful idea, Mother Goose," Marie said, and then nodded at the soldier. "Let them eat cake!"

I don't care what those stiff French aristocrats say about Marie Antoinette—a queen who parties like her is a queen I can get behind!

1775, Corsica

Dear Diary,

My suggestion didn't do Marie Antoinette any favors. Those French have really got it in for her! The whole country is a mess right now. They say a revolution is on the horizon. Everyone is so angry and pointing their fingers at everybody else. It reminds me a lot of the Salem Witch Trials—thank goodness I got out of *there* when I did!

I avoided all the chaos on the continent today and went to the island of Corsica to spread fairy tales. I knew I wouldn't find much there, but Mama needed some sun. All I found was a large fancy estate. I knocked and a bug-eyed housekeeper answered the door.

"Sorry to bother you, but are there any kids around here?" I asked.

"You must be the new tutor!" she said, then sighed with so much relief her posture sank a foot.

"Tutor? Nope. I'm afraid I'm not your girl," I said.

"Are you sure?" she asked desperately. "It pays five hundred francs a day!"

"Then I'm your girl!" I said quickly.

The housekeeper led me inside the estate to a drawing room that had been set up like a classroom. There was only one desk, and a small boy was pouting at it. His arms were crossed and he was sticking his lower lip out. I could already tell he was going to be a little hellion.

"Master Bonaparte?" the housekeeper said cautiously, treating the kid like he was a dangerous animal. "Your new tutor is here."

The boy instantly shot me a dirty look and I winced. He had a face only a mother could love.

"We've had a difficult time keeping tutors," the housekeeper whispered to me.

"No kidding," I said. "I bet you have a hard time keeping the wallpaper with a kid who looks like that."

The housekeeper left the room and promptly shut the door behind her. For a second, I was afraid I might be locked in. Had I been tricked? Was this kid about to eat me?

"So, what are they teaching you kiddos these days?" I asked him.

He just glared at me and stuck his lip out even more.

"You don't talk much, do you, um ... *Napoleon*," I said, reading the nameplate on his desk.

Still, the kid didn't say anything. I searched the classroom for something I could teach him and noticed a large globe of the Otherworld near the chalkboard. The boy dropped his arms and looked up at the globe mesmerized, like he had never seen anything so beautiful.

"How about some geography?" I pointed to France. "Do you know what this is, Napoleon?"

"*Mine?*" he said. I was surprised the little spawn could talk. He had a voice like an angry Chihuahua.

"*Close,* but you live *here* on the island of Corsica. Can you tell me what *this* is?" I said and pointed to Italy.

"*Mine?*" he said, and eerily raised an eyebrow.

"No," I said. "That's Italy. I had a good friend once who lived there. His name was Leonardo da Vinci. Maybe one of your old tutors taught you about him?"

The kid wasn't interested in anything but the map, so I decided to stick to it.

"How about this country?" I asked. "I'll give you a hint. It starts with an *E*."

"*Mine?*" he said. Maybe his previous tutors had only stuck around long enough to teach him one word?

"No, that's *Egypt*. What about this big one in the corner? Do you know what *that* is?" I asked, pointing to Russia.

A wicked little smirk grew on Napoleon's face.

"*Mine...,*" he whispered sinisterly to himself. It was so trippy, I was afraid his head would spin next.

"You'd better start raising an army now if you expect the whole world to be yours one day, Napoleon," I chuckled.

I don't think Napoleon realized I was kidding, because he suddenly dashed out of the classroom, knocking his desk over as he went. What a little creep. I'm going to ask for a raise.

1869, Washington, DC

Dear Diary,

The United States changes so much every time I visit it. Thank goodness that Sacagawea girl helped Lewis, Clark, and me explore the Northwest, otherwise the country never would have expanded so much. Hopefully the good old USA will expand socially as much as it has geographically.

Today I attended the women's suffrage convention with my pals Susan B. Anthony and Elizabeth Cady Stanton and many other brave women. Our friendship started a few years ago when I saw them protesting a town hall meeting with signs that said *Votes for Women*. I wasn't sure what this was all about, so I decided to get to the bottom of it.

Susan and Elizabeth took me out for dinner and explained everything they had been fighting for. I was shocked to learn women are seen as *secondary* to men in most places in the Otherworld, and in the United States they weren't even allowed to vote. Isn't that the most ridiculous thing you've ever heard of? Had I been aware of that sooner, I would have tried fixing it eons ago! I would have made my friend Benjamin Franklin put it into the Constitution—he was one of very few people in the 1700s who owed *me* money.

With so many incredible examples of intelligent, strong, and fearless female leadership (Queen Elizabeth, Catherine the Great, Queen Victoria, Maria Theresa—basically all my old friends!) you wouldn't think women would have to fight this hard just to *vote*! The whole thing is ludicrous.

I think the men trying to stop us are just afraid they'll lose their jobs because women will see right through their lies! I keep telling the girls, "In the

fairy-tale world, more women are in control than men, and it's in a lot better shape than this world!"

Every time I see a discouraged little girl, I tell her, "Don't worry, kid. By the time you're my age, not only will you be voting, but men will be voting *you* for president!"

1886, Texas

Dear Diary,

For the last eight months, Lester and I have been traveling the United States as part of Buffalo Bill's Wild West show. We've been attracting crowds by the thousands! It reminds me so much of my wrestling days. Sure, Annie Oakley might have top billing, but it's a thrill nonetheless. I've missed the adrenaline rush from performing dangerous acts in front of an audience.

We were gearing up for our first stint in Europe, and everyone was getting more excited each day. I couldn't wait to take the gang to all my favorite spots. However, the morning before our departure,

Bill came into my trailer and dropped a bombshell on me.

"Goose, there's no easy way to put this," he said. "The other performers and I have been talking, and we don't think it's a good idea that you join us in Europe."

"Bill, what do you mean? Lester and I are one of the best acts you've got!" I said.

"It's too much of a liability, Goose," he said. "Shooting bottles off the heads of children volunteers may be okay out here in the Wild West, but that's not going to fly in Europe."

"Is this about that mishap in Kansas? Because you know my aim has improved so much since then!" I said.

"It's not just the act, Goose," Bill said. "We're all getting a little tired of Lester. He's demanding, rude to the fans, eats all the food, and we all know he's not easy to travel with."

This isn't the first time I've been let go from a gig, and it won't be the last. Obviously, I was disappointed, but there was no use in fighting it. A good performer knows when it's time to take a bow.

"I guess this is good-bye, then," I said. "Take care of yourself, Bill. Please write to us when you reach the 1889 World's Fair."

"We will, Goose," Bill said. "And thanks for supplying us with all those empty bottles—you've got the liver of an ox."

Lester and I packed up our things and were gone by the afternoon. Can you believe out of all the gun-happy cowboys in Bill's circus, *I* was the liability? That's a first.

Our departure is probably for the best, though. I'm not sure how much longer Lester and I will stay in the Wild West. I've got dust in places I didn't know I had. If only my friend Jesse James was still around, we could start up a Wild West show of our own.

1938, South Pacific

Dear Diary,

Lester and I decided we deserved a break after spreading fairy tales throughout South America. So, we decided to find a nice private island in the South Pacific where no one would disturb us—and where the Fairy Council wasn't likely to find us. Apparently, we weren't the only ones with this idea.

We were flying over the Pacific Ocean when something shiny caught my eye on a desert island below. It was a silver plane that looked awfully familiar. We circled the island so I could get a better look at it. On the beach we saw a woman relaxing on a bamboo lounge chair. She sipped a coconut drink as she enjoyed the sun.

"Oh, my word! Lester, that's *Amelia Earhart*!"

It was a miracle! She had been missing for a year! The whole world thought she'd crashed into the ocean and died during her flight around the world. Lester and I dived toward the island and landed in the sand right beside her.

"Amelia! I can't believe it's you!" I said and embraced my old friend. "The whole world's been looking for you! I'm so glad you're alive."

Amelia wasn't as excited to see me as I was to see her. In fact, she looked a little embarrassed.

"Hi, Mother Goose," she said shyly. "Well . . . I guess you've caught me."

"What do you mean *caught you*?" It didn't take me long to understand what she was getting at—her plane was in perfect condition. "You didn't *crash* on this island, did you?"

"Not exactly," she said. "I'm sorry! I feel terrible that I made the world so worried, but I needed a break! I couldn't escape the pressure at home.

The press was constantly hounding me, photographers followed me everywhere, and no matter how many aviation records I set, no one was satisfied! Everyone only wanted me to do more— nothing was ever enough!

Staging a 'flight around the world' and faking my disappearance was the only way I could get a little *me time*. Please don't hate me?"

"Hate you?" I said. "I was gonna ask if I could pull up a chair!"

1942, England

Dear Diary,

I can't write too much today—the world's at war!
Lester and I are doing our part to fight the Nazis.
We've been asked personally by Winston Churchill
to lead the British Royal Air Force, so obviously I
have to keep the details to myself. Wish us luck!

It's a tough time in the Otherworld, but I've been
telling everyone to *keep calm, and carry on!* The
phrase has really caught on. It might be the best thing
I've said since *Jack and Jill*.

1954, HOLLYWOOD

Dear Diary,

I was in California today getting lunch with Walt Disney. He's been after the film rights to my life story for years. I keep telling him they're not for sale, but he still spoils me with meals and gifts in hopes that I'll change my mind. (Apparently, he's got his hands full with opening a theme park next year. I'd never say this to his face, but it sounds like a bust.)

I don't know how it happened, but I accidently stumbled into the offices of a director named Billy Wilder. He took one look at me and begged me to audition for the female lead of his new film, *The Seven Year Itch.*

A career in the film industry was something I never thought possible—there isn't enough light in the world to smooth my wrinkled face for a close-up. Mr. Wilder assured me I was perfect for the role and they had been searching for months to find an actress with my charm and charisma. How can you say no to that?

Mr. Wilder gave me the script and took me to the soundstage where they were shooting the screen tests. I don't want to jinx things, but I have to say *I nailed it*! Everyone was standing and applauding when I finished the first scene. Maybe Hollywood is ready for someone like me?

"Thank you so much, Ms. Goose!" Mr. Wilder said. "That was inspirational! We'll be in touch!"

I was feeling pretty cocky and had a new bounce in my step. I passed another actress waiting for a screen test on my way out. She was pretty and blonde— definitely not what they were looking for.

"Hate to break it to you, honey, but I think I got the part," I told her.

"Next! Miss Marilyn Monroe!" Mr. Wilder called out.

She gulped and headed into the soundstage. Poor thing. Some people just aren't Hollywood material.

1963, Washington, DC

Dear Diary,

It's been almost a century since I campaigned for women's suffrage, and yet I found myself in Washington, DC, today marching for rights. This time around I marched for civil rights with Dr. Martin Luther King Jr. and hundreds of thousands of other people.

It baffles me that in the Otherworld people are treated so differently just because of the color of their skin. In the fairy-tale world, there are all kinds of different skin colors (black, white, blue, green, red, yellow, orange, purple—every color you can imagine), but no one is treated any differently because of it. Learning about slavery was an even harder pill to swallow. That's something that barbaric creatures like trolls and goblins do; I couldn't believe human beings did it to one another here.

I've been around a long time and have seen a lot of things. One thing I've learned is that only in times of unity can there be progress. With so many obvious examples of this in history, why are so many still set on segregation?

It was such a spectacular day, and Dr. King gave a powerful speech that moved this old girl to tears, but it'll always be hard for me to understand the reason we were there. People shouldn't have to fight people just to be people. You'd think more people would get that.

1969, WOODSTOCK

Dear Diary,

I only have one word for you—*Woodstock*. Whoever came up with the concept of a *music festival* might the most brilliant person to walk the earth. Oh, wait—was that my idea? It's hard to remember (and hear) things today. If so, it's the single greatest contribution I may ever bring into this world. Forget Humpty Dumpty!

I wish I could tell you more about it, but what happens in Woodstock stays in Woodstock. There's no way Walt Disney can turn my life into a family movie after this week.

1970, Las Vegas

Dear Diary,

Tonight Lester and I met my friends Frank, Dean, Sammy, Peter, and Joey out for a drink in Vegas. Boy do those guys know how to make an old girl and her goose laugh! If you thought their movies were funny or their albums were nice to listen to, you've never heard them get together! It's wonderful having friends with just as many crazy stories as I do!

They call themselves the Rat Pack, but whenever I'm around, we're known as "The Goose Group." We've been toying around with the idea of starting a nightclub act and taking it on the road. I'm not sure that's a good idea, though—I'm wanted in almost thirty states, and Lester in fifteen. Maybe they'll settle for a residency in Vegas? Lester gives a mean fan dance when he's in a performance mood.

That reminds me, I never did get a call from Billy Wilder. The movie must have gotten canceled or was a total flop. They don't make them like they used to.

1976, Manhattan

Dear Diary,

Met my good friend Andy Warhol at some loft called the "Factory" in New York City today. It was exactly like I've always imagined the inside of his head to look—nothing but abstract art and outlandish characters running about.

We've been close for ages! When he got sick as a kid, I used to tell him stories and keep him company at the hospital. Andy's been an odd duck since birth, so naturally we hit it off right away. I'm so proud of him and everything he's accomplished. It takes real brilliance to turn eccentricity into something profitable.

Andy invited his friends and me over to unveil a new piece of art he had been working on. He ripped off the cover and for a moment I thought I had lost my mind. I saw the same picture of me but four times, each in a unique combination of colors. It was like the Fairy Council's worst nightmare.

"It's transcendent, don't you think?" he asked me. "I'm planning to do this for all my favorite people in pop culture, but no one will ever compare to you."

"Andy, if I'm honest, it's not my cup of tea," I said. "But then again, I told you painting canned food was a bad idea, and look what that did for you!"

I have to keep Lester home whenever I visit him. He's convinced Andy stole his hairstyle.

2015, WASHINGTON, DC

Dear Diary,

Well, I was back in Washington, DC, today, so you know what that means. . . . Yup, more marching! This time it was for marriage equality with my LGBT friends.

Of all the things I've protested over the years, I never thought I would be marching for the right to *love*. We never put limits on love where I come from— in fact, it used to annoy the crap out of me! Being among those men and women today made me realize how much I've taken that for granted.

I must say, of all the historical protests I've been to, this one was the most colorful and the most

fun, and had the best music! There were so many rainbows, I was reminded of the Fairy Council everywhere I looked. The LGBT community really knows how to protest something. Although I keep getting called *sir*, so I'm not sure what that's about.

You'd think I would be tired of marching after all these years, but I never back down from something I believe in. I've made a lot of mistakes in my time and committed many wrongs, but I'll always stand on the right side of history.

In Conclusion

What a life I've lived! As if it wasn't exhausting the first time around, reliving everything has really worn me out. From the looks of things, life isn't going to wind down anytime soon. I think this old lady has a few more adventures left in her. I've still got sights to see, people to meet, places to visit, and debts to pay off. . . .

It's funny to think about where I was before I found the Otherworld. I was unhappy, uninterested, and, worst of all, unappreciated. But just because my world had no use for this wise-cracking old lady doesn't mean there wasn't a world that did. And thank goodness I found it!

Think about all the people and places I would have missed if I hadn't gotten off my rocking chair and gone out into the world. Think about all the lives I touched and the changes I helped make—things sure would have been different if it weren't for me. True, the Otherworld may have been just fine without me, but we'll never know for sure.

The truth is, you'll never know the real differences you'll make in the world or in someone's life. Many people don't get the credit or the blame they deserve because history has a funny way of remembering things—always has and always will. All we can do is live every day *like we want to be remembered*, and hope it'll benefit the greater good. And if that's your goal, chances are you'll wind up helping someone along the way, even if it's just yourself.

Well, I better feed Lester before he gets crabby. All this reminiscing has made both of us very hungry. Thank you so much for taking the time to humor the life and times of this trailblazer. As my good friend Carol Burnett always says, "I'm so glad we had this time together."